# King
# Arthur

SCHOLASTIC JUNIOR CLASSICS

# King Arthur

adapted by
Jane B. Mason and
Sarah Hines Stephens

SCHOLASTIC INC.

New York   Toronto   London   Auckland   Sydney
Mexico City   New Delhi   Hong Kong   Buenos Aires

ISBN 0-439-44064-5

12 11 10 9 8                                  5 6 7 8/0

Printed in the U.S.A.                                  40
First printing, January 2003

# Contents

# King Arthur

# Prologue

LONG ago, on the island country we know as Britain, dark times reigned. Without laws or a good leader, the kingdom was being torn apart. Invaders landed daily on the island's shores. Instead of standing together to push the invaders away, the people fought amongst themselves. Over time, they grew more and more weak. Soon it seemed that all hope was lost.

The people of Britain fell into despair. No one had hope of a better life. But beneath the waters, under the trees, and in the caves, something was stirring. Magical forces were at work, conjuring hope and the promise of adventure. Mysterious whispers foretold a greater destiny for

Britain. The voices spoke of a glorious leader who would soon emerge and lead the country out of the dark times and into a new era.

The country's cries had not gone un-heard. The time of King Arthur was com-ing.

# Chapter 1

# The Sword in the Stone

KING Uther was dead — poisoned by an enemy. Now there was no strong leader to unite the people of Britain.

Dark times descended on the country. Knights and barons fought bitterly against one another. Raiders from foreign lands crossed the oceans in great numbers. They killed and enslaved innocent people, burned villages, and claimed the country as their own. Fear loomed over the land like a heavy cloud, darkening everything in its path.

While the people suffered and the countryside was ravaged, one man watched quietly: Merlin the Wise. Merlin was as old as Britain itself and had magic running through his veins. He could see the future as easily as another man could remember the past. Although the bloodshed and death in the land saddened him, he knew what was to come. A glorious future awaited Britain and its people.

Several months before, on the very day that King Uther's wife gave birth to the couple's only son, Merlin had gone to the king. King Uther and Queen Igraine were overjoyed by the boy's arrival, but their joy did not last long. Merlin had seen the future, and he immediately told Uther that the good king's death was not far away.

"And when you are gone, many will wish to slay your young son," Merlin explained. "But my Sight also shows me a way to save the boy. If you will entrust him to me I shall see that he is educated and well cared for even as he is hidden from those who wish to do him harm."

The king's face paled, but he was a brave man. "If my time is coming, then so be it," he told Merlin. "But I will not allow my son to be killed by the greed and fear of others. Take him, then, and keep him safe."

That very night, Merlin bundled up the baby and carried him out of the castle and down a secret path through the darkness. He traveled north for many days and knocked on the door of an old friend, Sir Hector. Sir Hector's wife opened the door. Merlin handed her the baby.

Merlin told his friends only that the boy's name was Arthur and that one day they would know the identity of his birth parents, but not today. Sir Hector and his wife were a kind couple with a five-year-old son of their own. They happily agreed to look after the orphan child and raise him with love. Merlin left the baby in their care. Then he retired to the valleys and forests of Wales to watch and wait.

It was not easy to watch. Wars tore the country apart. Friends turned against one another. Fear lived in everyone's heart. The smell of death and fire lingered in the air. Had Merlin not been a man who understood destiny, he might have brought Arthur out of hiding too soon. Fortunately, Merlin knew how to be patient.

By the time Arthur was sixteen years old, it seemed all hope of reuniting the country was lost. It was then that Merlin traveled to London to meet with the archbishop Dubricius. Even though Merlin and the archbishop were not of the same faith, they had great respect for each other.

"I bring good news," Merlin told the archbishop. "Soon the darkness that envelops us will disappear, and a true leader will emerge. He will rule over all of Britain as high king. You must gather all of the lesser kings and lords and knights of Britain at your cathedral on Christmas Day."

The archbishop was not entirely sure what Merlin meant, but he knew enough not to question him. He followed the wizard's instructions and sent for the kings and lords and knights. They came from the far corners of Britain and filled the pews of the cathedral. Each of them wondered why he had been summoned. None could have guessed the miraculous events that would come to pass.

In the middle of the sermon, a great commotion arose in the cathedral's courtyard. Stepping out into the cold winter air, the lords and their ladies were shocked to see a large piece of marble sitting in the center of the courtyard. On top of the marble was a black anvil. Stuck deep through them both was a glittering sword.

The stone, the anvil, and the sword were a shock to all, for they had not been there before the service. Even more surprising was the inscription carved in golden letters on the stone itself:

WHOEVER DRAWS THIS SWORD FROM THE STONE IS THE RIGHTFUL HIGH KING OF BRITAIN.

There was silence as everyone considered the significance of the inscription. Then the lords and knights began to shove their way forward for a chance to claim the sword and the crown. One after another, they pulled with all their might, but to no avail. The sword did not budge.

"We shall try again on New Year's Day," the archbishop told the men. "A great tournament will be held, and afterward you can try the sword a second time."

During the following week, knights traveled from far and wide to compete in the jousting tournament and try their hand at removing the sword from the stone. The London inns were filled to capacity, and the roads were crowded with visitors. Among them were Sir Hector and his two sons.

Kay, Hector's elder son, had grown up to be a powerfully built young man. He was thickly muscled and a bit thickheaded as well. Newly knighted, the young man was terribly proud of himself and eager to prove his strength and bravery in a joust. He was altogether the opposite of his foster brother.

Young Arthur had no intention of competing and no need to prove himself. He was a clever lad, and slightly built. Arthur thought it would be years before he was knighted, but he was not anxious. For now he was pleased to watch everything that happened and to serve as Kay's squire, even though lately the older boy had done nothing but bark orders at him.

On the way to the joust, Kay suddenly realized that he'd forgotten his sword. He was about to blame Arthur when Arthur took the blame himself.

"I should have made sure you had it," he confessed. "It's a squire's job to outfit his knight. I will retrieve it and meet you at the south end of the fields." Without another word, Arthur turned back toward the inn to retrieve the weapon.

Arthur hurried as quickly as he could, but there were hoards of people in the streets, all heading toward the tournament. The skinny boy felt like a fish swimming upstream. By the time he arrived back at the inn, everyone had left for the tournament. The doors and windows were shut and locked tight.

*What am I to do?* Arthur thought with a heavy heart. He honestly felt responsible that Kay had no sword. His brother had been looking forward to proving his honor on the fields. If he could not compete it would be Arthur's fault.

As Arthur turned back toward the jousting arena, he suddenly remembered a sword he'd seen in the cathedral courtyard. *I'll just borrow it for a bit,* he told himself. *After the tournament I can return it.*

Arthur had only glimpsed the sword in the stone from a distance and had not read the inscription. He was concerned with only one thing: getting Kay a sword as quickly as possible. So he didn't pause to read the gold letters before placing his hand on the sword's hilt. The handle felt strange and familiar at the same time, and Arthur removed the blade from the stone in a single graceful movement.

With the mighty sword in his grasp, Arthur raced off to the jousting fields. He found his brother at the south end and thrust the sword into his hands.

When Kay looked down at the sword, his face turned as pale as a ghost's. "Father," he whispered desperately to Sir Hector. "Father, this is the sword. I hold it in my very hands. It must be that I am the rightful king of all Britain."

Sir Hector stared at the sword, then at his son, and finally at Arthur. "We must go back to the cathedral," he said quietly.

Inside the cathedral, Sir Hector held a Bible before his son Kay. "Place your hand on this," he said, "and tell me how it is you came by the sword."

Kay scowled as his cheeks grew red with shame. But he could not disobey his father.

"Arthur brought it to me," he said quietly.

Sir Hector turned to look at his foster son. "Did anyone see you?" Hector asked.

"I do not think so," Arthur replied. He was not sure what was going on but had an uneasy feeling in his stomach.

"I would like you to put it back," Hector said, "and then draw it again."

Silently, the three returned to the courtyard, and Arthur replaced the sword as easily as he had pulled it out. Before he could draw it again, Kay threw himself in front of Arthur, grabbed the hilt, and yanked with all his strength.

The sword did not move.

Sir Hector placed a hand on his older son's shoulder, pulling him back. "Arthur," he said, "please draw the sword."

Arthur stepped forward, placed his hand on the sword's hilt, and deftly removed the blade from the stone.

As Hector gazed at the glimmering sword, a single memory flew into his mind. He saw Merlin at his table, sixteen years before, telling him that he would know in time who Arthur's true parents were. That time had come.

Sir Hector dropped to his knees, pulling Kay down beside him. "Arthur," he began, "you are my true king. It has been an honor to raise you as my son. I now vow to serve you until my death, as does Kay."

"Father, please get up!" Arthur begged, pulling on Sir Hector's arm. "A father should not bow before his son!"

Hector did not rise. Instead, he continued to speak. "When Merlin the Wise brought you to me, he did not tell me whose son you were. But now it is clear to me. Arthur, you are the child of King Uther and Queen Igraine, and the rightful high king of Britain."

Arthur's heart was filled with fear. What was Sir Hector saying? How could he be king? And yet, as he gazed into his adoptive father's eyes, part of him realized that all of it was true, that this was his destiny.

Sir Hector led Arthur to the archbishop and told him the story. Again Arthur was asked to remove the sword, which he did with ease. When the swarms of knights emerged from the jousting fields, they were given a second chance to pull the sword from the stone, as promised. None could move the sword.

Finally, after everyone had had a turn, Arthur stepped forward. For a fourth time he placed his hand on the hilt. A shiver snaked up his arm as he pulled the sword from the marble and anvil with no effort at all.

The crowd fell silent. Then words of doubt rippled through the mass of knights.

"A beardless boy," someone scoffed.

"Unknown bloodlines," grumbled another.

"Not capable of ruling," objected a third.

The knights were angry and jealous. But Merlin had expected this and had advised the archbishop accordingly. A new sword-drawing trial was set for Candlemas, when the knights would assemble next.

At Candlemas, the knights yanked and pulled as hard as they could, but still none could free the sword. Arthur removed the sword as easily as he had on New Year's Day. Still the crowd grumbled. Yet another trial was set, for Easter. Again, the knights were unsuccessful, while Arthur lifted the sword as if from butter. Finally, at Pentecost, the common people grew annoyed with the knights and their jealousy.

"Long live Arthur, for he is king," they shouted, falling to their knees. With much hesitation, the knights and lords dropped to their knees as well and mumbled allegiance.

Grudgingly, Arthur had been accepted as the new high king of Britain.

Chapter 2

# The Northern Revolt

ALTHOUGH Arthur was young, he was a good and honest king and a strong leader. As soon as his rule began he assembled armies and traveled across the country to set things right. He returned land and money to those who had it stolen from them. He punished those who had done the stealing. And he drove the Saxons and Danes from the land, giving it back to the British people. Before long, all of the counties in the south of Britain — as far north as the River Trent — were prospering and peaceful. That accomplished, Arthur built his capital at Camelot.

Camelot was a glorious place. Arthur had a generous spirit and welcomed everyone, rich or poor. Knights and poets and adventurers all came to his court. From the very start, the castle was filled with great feasting and gaming and merriment.

But the happy mood did not last long. Soon word came to Camelot that many of the lesser kings in the northern territories — the north of Britain and Ireland and Scotland and Wales — were planning a revolt against the high king. Arthur had shown the people that he was just and wise beyond his years. Still, the northern kings were furious that a beardless boy had claimed the throne. They did not believe that Arthur was in fact the son of Uther and Igraine. Why should they pledge to serve him?

Further news came that the rebels had amassed an army that was fifty thousand strong. Eleven kings — King Lot of Orkney, King Uriens of Gore, King Agwisance of Ireland, King Carados of Scotland, and seven more besides — were marching toward the high king.

Arthur was not afraid. Heeding Merlin's advice, he sent for two of his strongest allies, King Ban of Benwick and King Bors of Gaul. These men had been good friends to Arthur's father, King Uther.

It was not long before kings Ban and Bors arrived in Camelot with their armies. Arthur had been kept busy during those few days, for it was no small task to ready an army to march. There were supplies to be gathered, knights to be trained, and weapons to be sharpened and polished. A true leader, Arthur was as attentive to the supplies as he was to his fighting men. Finally, all was ready. Twenty thousand men marched northward to meet the hostile kings.

Twenty thousand is a good-sized army. Still, Arthur and his men were greatly outnumbered. The eleven lesser kings had no doubt been planning their rebellion since

Arthur had been crowned, and they had plenty of reinforcements. Arthur sent spies ahead, and word came back that the rebel army was camped just north of the River Trent. There was no sign that they knew Arthur was coming with his own weapons and knights. The high king had the element of surprise.

Arthur and his men attacked at first light, storming the misty rebel camp with weapons raised. It was a bloody battle. Horses reared up, knocking knights to the ground. Knights rushed at one another, wielding bludgeons. Swords flashed, glinting in the morning light as they tried to find flesh.

It was not long before the earth was stained with blood. Arthur himself was badly wounded, but he ignored the pain. He moved across the field, slashing the enemy and shouting orders to his men, encouraging them and urging them onward.

Men fell left and right, and still the battle raged on into the night. The ground was littered with the dead from both sides.

Finally, Merlin appeared on top of a hill overlooking the battlefield. The full moon shone behind him.

"Listen to what I have to say," he said, raising his arms into the air. The fighting stopped. "The time has come for you to stop battling amongst yourselves. Britain must unite under one leader. Arthur is the son of King Uther and Queen Igraine. He alone can lead the country to prosperity and peace. Fate has chosen him as your rightful king, and you all must pledge to serve him."

There was a moment of silence as the kings and soldiers considered Merlin's words. Their wounds still wet with blood, they lowered their weapons and looked down at the bodies of the fallen men. Many lives had been lost. And for what?

"Long live Arthur, our rightful king!" one of the lesser kings shouted, bowing before Arthur.

The soldiers and several other kings bowed as well. "We pledge to serve you until we die," they declared.

Only King Lot and King Carados would not pledge to serve the high king. Taking their last few bedraggled knights with them, they fled into the mountains from whence they'd come. Lot and Carados would never befriend King Arthur, but they made their peace with the high king many years later when King Lot and his queen sent their four sons to serve Britain as knights in King Arthur's court.

Although the battle had cost many lives, Britain's new day had finally begun. Arthur had proven himself the true high king of Britain.

# Chapter 3

# Excalibur

ARTHUR fought back the Saxons and defeated the northern kings with the very sword he had pulled from the stone to claim his crown. Now the young king felt that he and his sword should be given leave to rest a while at Camelot, to recover from their battles. But Arthur and his sword had not been long at his court when a young squire rode through the gates. He led behind him a second horse, with a slain knight slung across its back.

"Vengeance!" the boy cried to any who would listen. "Vengeance for my good master, Sir Miles."

The knights at court gathered around the boy to hear what had befallen the slain knight. Arthur nodded, and the squire's tale began.

"Nearby on the forest path there is a knight, Sir Pellinore, who challenges all who pass. My master fought fiercely and was killed unjustly," the squire said breathlessly. "He wanted only to pass. Is there no man here who will take up his cause?"

Many of the men circling the squire and his fallen master voiced their outrage that any would dare block the forest road. But it was a mere boy who stepped forward to accept the challenge.

His name was Griflet, and he was not yet a knight.

"My lord," Griflet appealed to the king, "I beg of you, make me a knight. I will ride out at once."

Arthur looked thoughtfully at the young squire before him. He was bold. If he lived he would make a fine knight.

"You are too young," Arthur said gently,

though the king was little more than a boy himself.

Yet Griflet did not step away. Instead, he looked the king in the eye, then bowed his head to accept the light touch of King Arthur's sword that would make him a knight.

Arthur was moved by the boy's resolve. Relenting, he touched Griflet's shoulders with the flat of his blade.

"Arise, Sir Griflet," Arthur spoke, "and promise me this: that you will ride against Sir Pellinore only once. Then you will return here to me."

The newly knighted Sir Griflet nodded to his king. Then he quickly took up his lance and shield, mounted his horse, and rode out of the courtyard in a cloud of dust.

How many times Arthur doubted his decision in the hours that followed he did not know. But the relief he felt when

Griflet rode back into the courtyard at Camelot was immeasurable. Arthur strode out to meet and welcome the new knight. Reaching up to clap the knight on the back, he saw the end of a lance sticking out of Griflet's side. Suddenly, the relief that had filled him was replaced by remorse. He had sent the boy out to his doom!

Griflet slid from his horse into the king's waiting arms. Arthur lowered him gently to the ground and asked that the court's best healers be sent for immediately.

"I have failed you, my lord," Griflet said weakly.

"It is I who have failed you," Arthur replied. He begged the boy not to waste his energy on speech, but Griflet was intent on telling his tale.

"I followed the forest road, not far, until I spied Sir Pellinore's shield hanging from a tree," he said weakly. "I hammered on the shield with the end of my lance to call the knight out. But he did not come. I hammered again, and the shield crashed to the ground. That is when I saw him.

"He burst from his tent like a demon, dark and bellowing.

"'Who dares strike my shield?' he asked." Griflet paused to catch his breath. "'I do,' I said. But the dark knight laughed at that, even when I told him that I had been knighted by King Arthur himself.

"He told me I was too young and green to be a match for him."

Hearing this, King Arthur's heart ached. That had been his fear as well.

Griflet went on. "He told me to stand down and live to fight another day. But I took up my lance. We rode against each other only once. I struck his shield with my lance and saw the dent it made before I was thrown from my horse. For a moment, I did not feel the damage he had done me."

Griflet's hand went to his side, where the shaft of Sir Pellinore's lance was lodged in his ribs. Beside him on the ground was his shield. A hole had been pierced through the center.

"I waited for Sir Pellinore to do me in. I could not draw my sword." Griflet panted. "He took my helmet off and laughed. Then, instead of a death blow he dealt me a compliment.

"'You do not lack courage,' he said. 'If you survive, you will surely be a great knight.' Then he lifted me into my saddle and pointed my horse toward home."

His tale told and the last of his energy spent, Griflet fainted in the king's arms.

Anger flared inside Arthur as he handed Griflet over to the healers' care. He was angry at Pellinore and angry with himself for allowing Griflet to accept such a difficult challenge.

Mounted on his best horse and wearing his strongest armor, with the visor on his helmet closed to hide his identity, the king rode out to face Sir Pellinore himself.

Like Griflet before him, Arthur found Pellinore's shield hanging from a tree. Also like Griflet, he struck it hard with the end of his lance.

"Who dares strike my shield?" Pellinore roared, throwing open the flaps of his tent.

"Who dares to bar the road challenging all who will pass?" Arthur countered from atop his horse.

"I do," Pellinore replied. "And if you wish to pass, then I will challenge you, too."

Arthur drew back, accepting the challenge. And when Pellinore was astride his own horse, the two men galloped toward each other. They met in a clash of metal and splintering wood. Both lances shattered. In an instant, the armored men were off their horses and drawing swords.

The blades came together again and again, ringing through the forest. The two men fought until both were bleeding and exhausted. Their armor was torn and dented, their breathing harsh beneath their helmets. Each mighty blow was met with its equal until at last Arthur struck with such force that his blade broke and he was left with only a jagged hilt.

"Yield." Pellinore panted, knocking Arthur to the ground and pulling off his helmet. "Beg for mercy or die." He raised his sword.

"I welcome death when it comes," Arthur replied, "but I beg mercy from no man."

Pellinore would have preferred for Arthur to yield. He had not battled such a worthy opponent in a long time, and he enjoyed a good fight. But he drew back his sword and prepared to take Arthur's life. At that moment, a tall figure stepped from behind the trees and laid his hand on Pellinore's sword.

"Would you kill the hope of all England?" Merlin asked, looking into Pellinore's startled face. "Would you slay your king?"

Before Pellinore could reply, Merlin the Wise pointed a pale finger at his brow. Pellinore crumpled to the ground, and the wizard bent to help Arthur to his horse.

"I am grateful for my life, Merlin, but I would rather die than win a fight this way," Arthur said. "Sir Pellinore is a valiant knight."

"He is in better health than you," Merlin replied. "He will awake in a few hours. And one day he will serve you well, as will his sons after him."

Relieved, Arthur slumped in his saddle and allowed Merlin to lead him to a healer deep in the woods. It was several days before the king was well enough to ride away from the healer's cabin. Even then he looked downcast.

"What troubles you?" Merlin asked, though of course he already knew.

"I have no sword," Arthur replied.

31

"Do not worry, my friend," Merlin said mysteriously. "Your old sword served you well. Now the time has come for you to take your true sword. A sword unlike any other."

Arthur was accustomed to Merlin's mysterious talk and followed the wizard deeper and deeper into the forest without question. At last the trees parted, and they came to the shore of a large lake shrouded in mist.

Merlin pointed out into the water. There Arthur beheld the strangest sight he had ever seen. A graceful arm, draped in white silk, stretched out of the water. In its grasp was a shining sword. Before Arthur could gather his wits, he saw something else. A maiden was walking toward him on the waters.

"Who is that?" Arthur whispered.

"That is the Lady of the Lake," Merlin replied plainly. "She's come to tell you how you may claim your sword."

The Lady came closer, until she stood before the king. Bowing low, she spoke to him with a voice like a clear stream. "Excalibur awaits." She gestured toward the golden sword. "I have guarded it for many years, waiting for you to claim it. Do you want it?"

Arthur nodded, and the Lady of the Lake pointed him toward a small boat he had not noticed before. He stepped aboard, and the boat glided soundlessly across the lake without sails or oars to propel it. When it drew alongside the arm bearing the sword, the boat stopped. Gently, Arthur reached out and took the sword. The moment it was in Arthur's grasp, the hand that had held it slipped silently under the surface, and the boat turned back to shore.

When Arthur stepped off the boat, the Lady of the Lake was nowhere to be seen. He held his new sword aloft, admiring it. It was finely made and had with it a jeweled scabbard that the king turned over in his hand.

"Which do you prefer, the sword or the scabbard?" Merlin asked as they turned their horses toward home.

Arthur laughed at the question. "The sword, of course."

"Then you are a fool," Merlin laughed back. "For the scabbard is worth ten swords. Take care to keep it close to you always, for when you wear it, no matter how wounded you become in battle, you will not lose a drop of blood."

As always, Merlin's words were wise, but Arthur was not listening to the warning. He was busy buckling on his new sword and dreaming of the adventures he would have with Excalibur at his side.

# Chapter 4

# Guenevere and
# the Round Table

THERE came a time of calm in Arthur's kingdom, and in that time Arthur's barons began to press him to take a wife. As in all things, Arthur sought Merlin's advice.

"Your barons are right." Merlin nodded, stroking his long beard. "You are past twenty, and you should marry. Your kingdom wants a queen. Tell me, Arthur, whom does your heart choose?"

Arthur thought for a long moment. He had seen many beautiful maidens in his adventures, but there was only one for whom his heart longed. "The Lady Guenevere, daughter of Leodegrance. I love her above all others," Arthur said. Even as he spoke of her he felt a calm, like a warm summer breeze, wash over him.

Merlin nodded again, more slowly this time. His heavy brows drew together. "Indeed, the Lady Leodegrance is fair," he said. "If you were not sure of your choice I could have found you another wife who would love you well. But I see your heart is already given and not easily retrieved. I will arrange the marriage."

Merlin traveled to the home of King Leodegrance at once. There, Arthur's proposal was happily received.

"Never before have I heard such welcome news." King Leodegrance beamed. "King Arthur is noble and good, and nothing would please me more than to see my daughter as his wife. In addition to my daughter's hand, I wish to give the king a gift to prize above all others. But what? He does not need land." Leodegrance paced the room for a moment, then stopped short. "The Round Table!" he cried, clapping his hands together. "I shall give Arthur the Round Table. After all, it was given to me by his own father, Uther Pendragon."

Merlin smiled at the news, for he knew that the Round Table would complete Arthur's court. When both the Lady Guenevere and the great table were ready to travel, he escorted them back to Camelot.

By the time they arrived at court, preparations for the wedding were nearly complete. The great hall was strung with banners, and the church was decorated with garlands and ribbons. Guenevere was radiant in white-and-gold robes as she stepped to meet her king. Everyone agreed that Arthur had chosen a perfect queen.

After the wedding ceremony, there was a second ceremony to crown the queen. A golden band was placed on Guenevere's head. Then the entire court went back to the castle to celebrate.

When the king and queen entered the great hall where the Round Table had been placed, they were compelled to stop and marvel. The table was so enormous it almost filled the huge room. And standing around it were some of the finest knights ever assembled.

In addition to the Round Table itself, King Leodegrance had sent to Arthur one hundred of his best knights. But even that great number was not enough to fill the places at the table. So before the wedding, Arthur had asked Merlin to choose fifty more worthy knights. He had done so, and now the room was filled with valiant men waiting to take their places at the table.

The knights lined up, bowing before the king and queen in turn. Each of them swore loyalty to Arthur the high king. As each knight made his pledge, his name appeared in gold letters on the back of a chair: Sir Hector, Sir Kay, Sir Gawain, Sir Accolon, and more. As the names appeared, each knight took his rightful place at the Round Table.

Soon the room was filled with joyful noise. Knights clapped one another on the back in congratulations and raised glasses to their lord and his new bride. Squires came in to fill plates, and bards began to tune their strings.

All fell silent when Merlin stood. "Sir knights of the table round, look about you, for this table is more wondrous than you know. There is none at this table who sits higher or lower, closer to the head or the foot than any other. Here every man is equal."

Merlin gestured for Arthur to sit at the Round Table with his knights. When the king took his place he noticed for the first time that a number of seats remained empty. "Who shall fill those seats?" he asked.

"One is for Sir Pellinore, the knight who nearly bested you in battle," Merlin explained. "Another is for Pellinore's son who is not yet born. The one beside you is for Sir Lancelot, son of your ally, King Ban, and soon to be your finest knight."

Still more chairs remained unfilled. With a start, Arthur realized that there would always be empty seats at the Round Table. Many knights would die in his service and many more would be waiting to take their place. It was a sobering thought, but Arthur could not dwell on it for long.

Out in the courtyard there came a loud ruckus, followed by a pounding on the doors.

The doors were flung open, and Sir Pellinore clanked into the hall, still dressed in his armor. Clumsily, he dropped to his knee before Arthur and swore his loyalty to the king.

"It is good to see you again." Arthur greeted his old foe and helped him to his feet. "And good to have you on my side."

Pellinore laughed, and the jovial mood returned to the hall. By the time he took his seat, the gold letters spelling out his name had already appeared on the chair's high back.

Arthur stood then and welcomed all of the knights to the Round Table. Before they ate he asked them to swear to a code of honor he had been thinking of for some time: that each knight would be just, merciful, and chivalrous, and that none would ever battle without cause or for personal gain. The knights swore to the code of honor, then lifted their glasses together, sealing the brotherhood.

During the toasting and celebrating, Merlin came and stood behind Arthur's chair. His wise black eyes looked around the great hall — at the knights, the ladies, King Arthur, and the Round Table. All of this he had had a hand in creating, and now his work was done. It was time for him to leave Camelot. He silently bid Arthur good-bye, and Arthur knew at once that he would not see Merlin again for a long, long time. This saddened Arthur greatly, but he knew that like everything else around him, it was part of his destiny. He took Merlin's hand for a moment, thanked him without words, then watched his great friend and adviser leave the hall and walk out into the starry night.

Arthur felt Merlin's absence immediately but took heart in the fine knights who filled almost all the seats at his Round Table. As time passed, Arthur learned to rule without Merlin. During Arthur's reign, the names on the backs of chairs at the Round Table would become known throughout the world for their fine deeds and adventures.

# Chapter 5

## The Dark Magic of Morgana le Fay

BEFORE Arthur's mother was married to Arthur's father, she was married to another man. King Goloris was kind enough, but he was old. Igraine was not in love with him.

Igraine raised three daughters with King Goloris: Morgause, Elaine, and Morgana le Fay. Later, Igraine fell in love with Uther, and they conceived Arthur. When Arthur was born, he had three half sisters who were already powerful queens, as was his own mother. Morgause had married King Lot of Orkney. Elaine had married King Netres of Garlot. And Morgana, the youngest, had married King Uriens of Gore.

It was Morgana who would bring the most trouble to Arthur. For she had adored her father, Goloris, and blamed Arthur's father for his death. Now that Uther was dead, too, she turned her bitterness toward Arthur.

Many times Merlin had warned Arthur that Morgana intended to hurt him. But Arthur loved his half sister and welcomed her and King Uriens to his court. They came often and frequently stayed a fortnight or more.

During one such visit, Arthur decided to go hunting with King Uriens of Gore and Sir Accolon of Gaul. They rode hard through the forests, chasing after a great stag. But the stag was swift, and soon the riders found themselves more than a dozen miles from Camelot. Still, the stag raced on.

The men were enjoying the chase considerably. They pressed their tired horses onward over hill and swamp. Finally, the horses fell beneath them and were unable to get up. The stag was just ahead, so the men decided to continue on foot.

Again the fleet-footed animal seemed impossible to catch. And now, for the first time, Arthur and his companions regretted that they had become so caught up in the chase. Fortunately, the stag was exhausted as well. It soon stopped at the edge of a lake for a drink. Arthur had just drawn Excalibur when the animal collapsed, dead.

The three lords raced forward to examine their prize. It was a worthy animal indeed, with mature horns jutting out of its great head. Then, as they stood together at the edge of the water, a sailing ship approached the shore. Draped with silk sails, it drifted silently across the still waters and stopped not five feet from the men.

"Come, let us go aboard," Arthur said,

for he was never one to ignore an adventure that came his way.

The three men stepped onto the boat and instantly heard tinkling laughter. A beautiful damsel appeared, followed by eleven others.

"Welcome, King Arthur," she said. "We have awaited you."

The maidens led Arthur and the others belowdecks to a cabin fitted with a large table and several chairs. The table was laid with delicious food and wines, and an intoxicating aroma filled the air.

Arthur and the men were very tired and hungry, so they immediately sat down. They ate and drank their fill, marveling at each delectable morsel of bread and meat and every thirst-quenching drop of wine. For though Arthur was king and accustomed to being well fed, he had never tasted anything as delicious as this food or as flavorful as this wine.

After they had eaten and drunk their fill, the men were led to three private cabins. Each man lay down on a bed as soft as a summer breeze and promptly fell asleep. None of them awoke or even stirred before daylight.

When the sun rose the next morning, King Uriens awoke to find himself in his bed at Camelot. His wife, Morgana, lay next to him, sleeping. But the corners of her mouth were turned up in a clever smile as if she had been up to some trick that only she knew about. Knowing that his wife was a powerful sorceress, King Uriens kept silent.

Arthur was not so lucky. He awoke on the cold floor of a dungeon, surrounded by a dozen moaning and imprisoned knights. Arthur sat up, wondering how he came to be in this place.

"Who are you?" he called to the men. "And why do you complain so severely?"

"We are prisoners of the lord of this castle," one of the men explained in a weakened voice. "He is Sir Damas, a most evil knight. He refuses to share the inheritance with his own brother, the good Sir Onslake. Sir Onslake has offered to fight his brother for his lands, but Sir Damas refuses. We have come as emissaries for Sir Onslake, but Sir Damas would neither listen to nor fight against us. He has imprisoned us all, some for more than seven years. Surely, we are to rot away here, for we can find no way out."

Arthur was pondering this injustice when a maiden came into the dungeon.

"How fare thee?" she asked the king.

"I do not know," said Arthur. "For I know not why I am here or what is to become of me."

The maiden smiled a small smile. "The

choice is yours," she said. "You can stay here, a prisoner forever, or you can agree to fight tomorrow in a duel for the lord of this castle. He has chosen you to be his champion."

Arthur hesitated for a moment. If what the imprisoned knight had told him was true, then fighting for Sir Damas was not a worthy cause. But he could not sit and rot in prison, either. And perhaps, if he agreed to fight, he could help these imprisoned men.

"I would rather fight than spend the rest of my days in darkness," he said. "But if I am to be champion for Sir Damas, then these men must be freed as well."

Now the maiden paused. "Very well," she finally said. "It is done."

"I need only a horse and armor," Arthur said. "Then I will be ready."

"You shall have both," the maiden promised, "the best in all the land."

As Arthur looked up at her, he suddenly

thought he had seen her before. "You look familiar," he said. "Mayhap you have been to Camelot?"

The maiden shook her head quickly. "No, no," she said. "I am the daughter of Sir Damas and have never ventured from this castle."

Arthur had no reason to suspect that the maiden was lying, but she was. For she was actually a lady-in-waiting to Morgana le Fay.

While Arthur was speaking to the maiden, Sir Accolon was waking from his own deep sleep. He was not in a bed, either, but was lying at the edge of a deep well. Had he so much as turned in his sleep he would have plunged to his death. When Sir Accolon realized this, he cursed the maidens on the ship. For he knew that they were not simple maidens but creations of an evil spell.

"May the heavens save Arthur, and

King Uriens as well," Sir Accolon muttered. And he vowed to slay all witches and enchantresses he came across from that day forward.

Sir Accolon was about to rise to his feet when an ugly dwarf appeared. The dwarf had a fat, flat nose and a large gash of a mouth.

"I am a messenger for Morgana le Fay," the dwarf explained in a hoarse voice.

Hearing Morgana's name caused Sir Accolon to listen intently, for he had loved her in secret for many years. The mere mention of her name caused his heartbeat to quicken in his chest.

"Morgana asks that you be her champion in a duel tomorrow at noon, against a man who has wronged her greatly. And so that you can do so without the loss of much blood, she sends the king's sword, Excalibur. If you truly love her, you will fight to the end and show no mercy."

Sir Accolon took the sword, marveling

at its razor-sharp blade and jewel-encrusted scabbard. It struck him as strange that she should send him another man's sword. But he knew the power the sword held and thought King Arthur would not mind him using it this one time, to defend his own sister's honor.

"Tell Morgana that she has found her champion," Sir Accolon told the dwarf. "And a true champion I shall be, to the death."

The next day, just before noon, Arthur and Sir Accolon were waiting at opposite ends of a large field. Each man had been assisted by half a dozen squires, wore full armor, and was mounted on a warhorse.

While the crowd gathered, each man lowered his visor to cover his face. The horses stomped their feet, impatient for the duel to begin. And then a maiden carrying a large sword appeared before Arthur.

"Your sister Morgana has sent your sword and scabbard so that you may be victorious in battle," she said.

Arthur leaned over and accepted the sword from the maiden. Unbuckling the sword he had been given by the squires, he fastened his own Excalibur to his waist — or so he thought.

Finally, it was time for the duel to begin. Arthur and Sir Accolon raised their lances and charged forward. The horses raced toward each other with such speed that both men were hurled to the ground with the first strike. Quickly scrambling to their feet, they drew their swords and continued to battle.

Arthur struck his opponent with forceful blows. Yet for some reason his sword did not seem to draw blood. And Accolon was a fierce opponent, ready with his own attacks. Soon, Arthur had several gaping wounds, his blood spilling to the ground.

The crowd watched, transfixed by the

bloodiness of the battle. They half expected Arthur to drop dead at any moment, for he was losing a great deal of blood. An ordinary man would no longer have had strength to fight.

Arthur ignored his wounds and struck again and again. As his strikes continued to draw almost no blood, it occurred to him that something was wrong. All of a sudden, he knew that the sword he held was not Excalibur at all but an imitation. The true Excalibur was in his opponent's hand.

This realization infuriated Arthur, and he charged Accolon with greater force than ever before. His sword hit Accolon hard on the side of his helmet, nearly sending Accolon to the ground. But the force of the blow was too much for Arthur's unworthy sword, and it broke into several pieces, which scattered across the bloodstained earth. Only the hilt remained in Arthur's hand.

Panting, Accolon got to his feet. "You have lost much blood this day, and you are unarmed," he said breathlessly. "Yield to me, and I shall not kill you."

"No!" Arthur declared firmly. "I would rather die a hundred deaths than forfeit my honor, as you will if you slay a weaponless man."

"I have vowed to battle until death," Accolon replied, raising his sword. He rushed full force at Arthur. But Arthur stood ready, took the blow evenly on his shield, and fought back with his swordless hilt.

Surprised, Accolon stumbled. While he was getting to his feet, the wind whistled in the air, rustling the nearby trees. Some say that Merlin was working an enchantment of his own. Others say it was the doing of the Lady of the Lake. Regardless, when Accolon went to strike a fatal blow to King Arthur, Excalibur merely jabbed into the ground, quivering near Arthur's feet. The scabbard Accolon wore fell from his waist to the bloody ground.

Arthur saw his chance. He quickly snatched up the scabbard, then pounced on the sword. "You have been from me too long," he told the weapon as he pulled it from the earth. "And have done much damage."

His true sword in hand, Arthur renewed the fight, slashing at Accolon so fiercely that blood spurted from his body, nose, and mouth.

"Yield or be killed," Arthur said.

"You might as well slay me," Accolon said, "for I am bound to fight until death, and you are the strongest knight I have ever battled. I will soon die from these wounds."

All at once, Arthur was filled with a sense of dread, for now the knight's voice sounded familiar. The past two days flashed in his mind — the hunt, the enchanted ship, the false weapon.

"Tell me, knight," he said, "who are you?"

"I am Sir Accolon, of King Arthur's court," Accolon replied.

Arthur gasped and fell to his knees. This was the worst wound he had received all day: He had been fighting his own knight!

"Tell me," Arthur said quietly, "who gave you the sword?"

"Morgana le Fay," Accolon replied. "She sent it to me and requested that I be her champion against a man who had wronged her. Now I see that I am to die by this sword. Pray tell me, who are you that Morgana wants killed so badly?"

"Oh, Accolon," Arthur cried, "I am Arthur, your king."

Now it was Accolon's turn to cry out. "Forgive me, sire," he begged. "On my honor I did not know it was you."

"You are forgiven," Arthur said. "The blame is not yours. For it is my sister's own evil that has caused us to fight this day."

Accolon nodded, then fainted upon the ground. Arthur wearily got to his feet and called Sir Damas before him.

"You, Sir Damas, are a villain and a dishonorable knight," he said. "I take from you all of your possessions save your castle, where you will live with nothing but your own cruel heart. All that you own — your servants and riches and lands — I give to your brother, Sir Onslake."

Arthur leaned heavily on his sword. His wounds were still bleeding and his speech had tired him. Then he, too, fell to the ground, fainting.

King Arthur and Sir Accolon were taken to a nearby abbey. There the two men's wounds were carefully tended with balms and salves. Arthur began to recover well, but Accolon had lost so much blood in the battle that he died the next day. A grieving Arthur had Accolon's body placed upon a silver horse. Guarded by six knights, it was sent to Morgana le Fay.

"Tell her this is the damage she has done," Arthur told the knights. "And tell her, too, that I once again have Excalibur. She will soon feel its blade."

When Accolon's body and Arthur's message arrived at Morgana's castle, Morgana flew into a fury. She quickly plotted an evil scheme to get Excalibur for herself.

That very day Morgana traveled to the abbey where King Arthur rested. Although the nuns told her the king was not to be disturbed, they did not have the courage to go against his own sister's will. "I will not wake him, but just sit with him awhile," she promised. So they let her in to see him while he slept.

Morgana saw immediately that she would not be able to take the sword from her brother, for he grasped it tightly even in sleep. But the scabbard lay unprotected at the foot of Arthur's bed. Morgana took the jeweled scabbard and hid it beneath her robes. Carrying it from the abbey, she mounted her horse and raced across the countryside until she came to a large lake. She hurled the scabbard into the air and watched it fall toward the water. But just before the scabbard struck the surface, a miraculous thing occurred. An arm clad in white silk reached up and caught it. Then the arm and the scabbard disappeared beneath the surface. King Arthur's scabbard was never seen again.

## Chapter 6

# Sir Lancelot of the Lake

OF the many knights of the Round Table, one stood out above the rest. His name was Lancelot of the Lake.

Lancelot was the youngest son of Queen Helen and King Ban of Benwick, Arthur's great friend and ally. But Lancelot was born during troubled times, and his parents died soon after his birth. Fortunately for Lancelot, the Lady of the Lake witnessed his parents' death in a vision, for she had the Sight. She came from her home under the lapping waves to gather the wailing child in her arms. Holding him tightly, she made her way back under the water to her glorious castle.

Lancelot was raised beneath the waters

as the Lady of the Lake's son. As such, he was treated like a prince. He learned to read and write and practiced the knightly arts. Then, when Lancelot was just eighteen, the Lady of the Lake told him it was time for him to leave her castle.

"You shall become a knight of the Round Table," the Lady of the Lake told him. And she gave him an intricate ring set with a beautiful purple stone. "This ring will keep you safe from enchantments," she told him. "Wear it always."

Lancelot was filled with both sadness and excitement as he bade the Lady of the Lake good-bye. "I will," he vowed.

Merlin had told Arthur of Lancelot's coming, so his arrival was not a surprise. Arthur felt a strong connection to the boy and loved him immediately. Even though Lancelot was young and untried, Arthur knew that Lancelot would become a champion of the Round Table. Arthur quickly made Lancelot a knight.

Other knights were not pleased by this. Most of them had worked hard to prove themselves to their king before they earned their knighthood. They wondered why this boy should be knighted without first being tested. Lancelot ignored the grumblings of the other knights. He did not care what others thought. In friendly jousts, Lancelot easily bested every knight. In swordplay his skill was unmatched. Before long, his reputation spread throughout Arthur's lands. People began to say he was the best knight in the world. Now the knights of the Round Table respected him. But Lancelot wanted to know himself if he was truly worthy of knighthood. And so, after residing at Camelot for a very short time, Lancelot went and kneeled before his king.

"I wish to ride out in search of adventure," he said.

The king smiled down at the boy, remembering when he, too, was eager to prove himself. "Permission granted," he said.

The next morning, Lancelot rode out with his cousin Lionel, another knight who had also asked permission to leave. They rode fast across the countryside until the noonday heat made them weary.

"Let us stop for a rest under this apple tree," said Lancelot. The tree's boughs were heavy with fruit, and the grass beneath the tree was soft and cool.

The men climbed off their horses, and as soon as Lancelot's head touched the ground he fell fast asleep. Lionel, however, was not tired. At once he was on his feet, gazing over the crest of a hill at a lush green valley that spread out before him. There he saw three knights riding hard, swirling up clouds of dust.

A moment later, it became clear why the knights were riding so fast. Behind them came a fourth knight, much bigger than the other three and clad entirely in blackened armor. The dark knight soon caught up to the other three, knocking each man from his horse in turn. Then he tied the first knight's hands with his reins and threw him across his horse.

"I must go help those three knights," Lionel said to himself. Leaving Lancelot sleeping, he quietly mounted his horse and rode away.

Lionel caught up to the dark knight just as he was throwing the third knight across his mount.

"Hold, sir," said Lionel, "and tell me why you treat these knights so shamefully."

"That is not of your concern," said the dark knight. "Yet I shall tell you that these are knights of King Arthur's court, and I treat them as I treat all of Arthur's knights."

"Not so," said Lionel, "for I am also a knight of Arthur's court, and I shall do battle with you to free these men."

So the two knights prepared to do battle, riding a fair distance apart. They charged and met each other with such force that the ground trembled beneath them. Lionel's spear was smashed to pieces, while the spear of the dark knight pierced Lionel's armor, sending him from his horse. Lionel landed so hard on the ground that the world went dark around him. Not wasting a moment, the dark knight bound Lionel's hands with his reins and threw him over his horse. Then, prodding all four of the horses in front of him, the dark knight made his way toward his castle.

Meanwhile, at Arthur's court, Lancelot's brother, Sir Ector, had decided to follow his cousin and brother on their adventure. But he took roads and paths different from Lancelot and Lionel's, and though he ended up in the same valley he did not pass by the apple tree where Lancelot slept. So when he came upon a woodsman, he asked, "Have you seen two knights riding this way, one with white armor and one with red?"

"I have not," replied the woodsman.

"Is there an adventure to be found near here?"

"Yes," said the woodsman. "But it is a difficult one, for none has succeeded in it. If you follow this road, you will come to a castle surrounded by a large moat. In front of the moat is a hawthorn tree, and hanging from the tree is a brass basin. If you strike that basin with your spear, you will come face-to-face with an adventure."

"I shall do so," said Sir Ector, and he rode onward. He did not know it, but the woodsman spoke of the castle of Sir Turquine, the same dark knight who had felled his cousin Lionel and led him away with the other three knights.

Sir Turquine was one of the most fearsome knights in all of Britain. His dungeon was always filled with knights and ladies. Some of these imprisoned knights and ladies Turquine held for ransom, then freed when the price was paid. But the knights of Arthur's court simply wasted away in the cold, dismal darkness. And that was where Lionel lay, though of course Sir Ector did not know this.

It was not long before Sir Ector came to a large hawthorn tree standing before an enormous castle built of gray stone. Just as the woodsman said, a brass basin hung from one of the tree's branches.

Sir Ector banged on that basin with his spear, and Sir Turquine appeared, armored in black and riding a black horse.

"Who beats upon my basin?" Sir Turquine bellowed, brandishing his spear.

"I do," replied Sir Ector plainly. He rode fast at the dark knight, drew his sword, and struck him so hard that Sir Turquine's horse spun twice around.

"Ha!" cried Sir Turquine. "That is the best blow ever to be dealt to me!" He urged his horse forward and grabbed Sir Ector under the arms, lifting him clean out of his saddle. Flinging Sir Ector across his own saddle, he galloped up to his castle.

Inside the courtyard, Sir Turquine threw Sir Ector to the ground. "You are the best knight I have done battle with," he said. "If you will serve me, I shall spare your life and pay you handsomely for your services besides."

"Never!" cried Sir Ector. For he would rather have died a hundred honorable deaths than serve one dishonorable knight.

"The choice is yours," Sir Turquine declared. And he had Sir Ector stripped of his armor and cast into his dungeon with the other knights.

Although Sir Lionel believed Lancelot to be asleep under the apple tree, a strange adventure had befallen him as well. For while he slumbered, Queen Morgana le Fay, who had left for the countryside to avoid King Arthur, happened to pass by and find him there. Queen Morgana recognized him at once because of her magic powers. Looking down at Lancelot's sleeping form, she immediately saw an opportunity to do harm to her brother, King Arthur. For it was already known throughout the land that Arthur loved Sir Lancelot and favored him above all of his knights.

Morgana climbed off her horse and quietly made her way to where Lancelot slept. But when she saw the purple stone upon his finger she knew she could not weave an evil spell around him, for it would not hold. So instead, she merely deepened his sleep and had him carried to her castle by several of her squires.

When Lancelot awoke, he was surprised to find himself in a richly decorated room. Before him stood a young damsel carrying a tray of food.

"How do you fare?" she asked.

"I do not know," replied Lancelot. "For I do not know if I am among friends or enemies."

The damsel set down the tray of food and gazed into Lancelot's eyes. "I am sorry to tell you that you are in the castle of Morgana le Fay, and she intends to do you no good. Pray, keep your guard against her and all those who dwell here."

"I shall do so," said Lancelot. "Thank you for your honest words."

The damsel left Lancelot alone in the chamber, but he was not alone for long. Soon Morgana appeared, dressed in golden cloth and wearing glittering jewels. "Welcome, Sir Lancelot," she greeted him. "It is indeed an honor to have you here with us."

Lancelot bowed graciously and smiled at Morgana. "Thank you, my lady, and for my delicious supper and fine surroundings. But can you tell me how I came to be here?"

Morgana smiled like a cat and replied, "My party and I found you sleeping alone under an apple tree, and I knew immediately who you were. I thought it would be nice to have the pleasure of your company in my own castle. So I brought you here and hope that you will stay with us for a few days."

"I should be glad to if I were not eager to go and search for my cousin Lionel," replied Lancelot. "For he was with me when I fell asleep, and I do not know what has befallen him, nor him of me."

"It shall be as you desire," said Morgana, a gleam in her golden eye. "But pray leave me a token so that I can be assured of your return." She removed from her finger a large gold ring set with several stones. Handing it to Lancelot, she said, "Let us exchange rings, this one for your purple-and-gold one. Then when you return we can exchange back again."

Lancelot shook his head. "That I cannot do, for I am sworn to wear this ring while there is breath in my body."

Queen Morgana's face reddened. "It is but a small request, made to you by a lady and a queen. And now, as the sister of King Arthur, I demand that ring from you."

Again Lancelot refused. "I may not give this ring to you, though I feel badly for refusing you what you wish."

Morgana's eyes flared like sparks from a fire as she got to her feet. Thrusting her ring back onto her finger, she turned on her heel and stormed from the room.

Left alone, Lancelot fretted, for he knew that going against Morgana le Fay was a dangerous thing to do. When darkness fell, he willed himself to stay awake so that none could do ill to him while he slept.

In the middle of the night, Lancelot

heard a soft rustling outside the chamber door. A moment later, the door opened, and the damsel who had brought him his supper appeared.

"I wish to help you," she said, "and to leave this place myself. I can help you escape from this castle. But in return I would ask of you one favor."

"What would you have of me?" asked Lancelot.

"My father, King Bagdemagus, has set a tournament one week from today. It shall be against the king of North Wales, who has three knights of the Round Table on his side. I request that you fight on my father's side so that he may win the tournament, for I hear that you are the greatest knight in the world."

"Lo!" said Lancelot. "I know your father to be a good and honorable knight. I would happily lend my aid to him at this tournament."

"Then I shall return shortly and lead

you from this place," the damsel said. And so she did, freeing Lancelot from the clutches of Morgana le Fay.

As soon as Lancelot was free, he donned his armor and went in search of Sir Lionel. He rode for several days until he finally came across a woodsman.

"Have you seen a knight bearing a red shield traveling these parts?" Lancelot asked.

"That I have not," replied the woodsman.

Lancelot was disappointed by this, for the woodsman was the first person he had come across since leaving the castle of Morgana le Fay. So he decided to ask one more question.

"Pray, good sir, is there an adventure to be had near here?"

"Aye, there is," said the woodsman. "But it is a dangerous one, for none has succeeded in it. If you follow this road you will come to a castle surrounded by a large moat. In front of the moat is a hawthorn tree, and hanging from the tree is a brass basin. If you strike that basin, an adventure you will have."

"Thank you, sir," said Lancelot. "I shall go in search of this castle and this tree and this basin." Lancelot did so, and when he found them he banged upon the basin very loudly. When the ringing of the basin grew quiet, Lancelot heard a great commotion in the castle. But no one emerged. So he banged on the basin again, and over and over again, until the bottom of the basin fell to the ground. Still, no one came.

Finally, Lancelot saw a giant knight riding toward him from the opposite direction. He was clad all in black and rode a black horse. In front of him was another horse and rider, only this rider was tied to his horse like a sack of grain. And lo! The bound rider was none other than Sir Gaheris, a knight of the Round Table!

"Sir!" Lancelot shouted, anger bubbling inside him. "Unbind that wounded man, for no knight deserves to be treated so!"

"I treat all knights of the Round Table this way," replied the dark knight. "I keep my dungeon full of them. And you shall be treated no differently, if you are from the Round Table as well."

"I am," said Lancelot. "And I am here to do battle with you."

Sir Turquine unbound Gaheris and set him down to watch the battle. Then he and Lancelot rode a good distance apart, turned, and charged each other. Crash! When their horses and spears and shields came together it shook the heavens like a booming thunderclap. The horses fell at once to the ground, and the knights leaped from their backs so as not to be crushed.

Lancelot and Turquine drew their swords and rushed at each other like two wild animals. Swords flashed in the sunlight. Each man was wounded whenever a weapon found its target. Indeed, the blows were so fierce that both men's armor began to break apart. Soon the ground was red with blood and littered with pieces of armor.

"Hold your sword!" Turquine suddenly called out. "I have a favor to ask. Let me go to the water and drink, for it is hot and I am thirsty."

"Drink, then," Lancelot replied, lowering his sword.

Sir Turquine drank. Then he took up his sword once more, coming at Lancelot with even greater fury than before. Lancelot fought off these blows as best he could but was wounded nonetheless. Then he, too, wished for a drink.

"Hold your sword, for now I am thirsty and would like a drink."

"I shan't," replied Sir Turquine, "and nor shall you."

Lancelot stared hard at Sir Turquine, fury building inside him. He had allowed his opponent a long drink but was now being denied the very same thing.

Casting aside his shield, Lancelot held his sword in two hands. He then charged the giant knight and struck him again and again, drawing upon every last bit of his strength. Finally, Sir Turquine fell to the ground and lay still.

The battle completed, Lancelot went to the water and drank. Then he untied Sir Gaheris and hugged him like a brother.

"Pray, go to yonder castle and free all who are imprisoned there," Lancelot said. "Tell them all to return to Camelot and that I will join them there as soon as I can."

Gaheris's eyes registered concern. "Surely you are not going to ride onward," he said, "for you are sorely wounded and your armor needs repair."

"I shall rest at an abbey not far from here," Lancelot replied. "And no doubt my armor can be mended there as well."

Gaheris could tell that there was no swaying Lancelot, so he hugged him good-bye and started toward the castle.

Lancelot, for his part, rode the rest of the day before coming to the abbey. The damsel from Morgana le Fay's castle was there to greet him, and she helped him from his horse. For four days Lancelot rested, and the damsel saw to his wounds most tenderly. She sent his armor to an armorsmith, and it was soon mended. On the fifth day, they journeyed to the castle of the damsel's father, King Bagdemagus.

"Thank you for coming," Bagdemagus told Lancelot. "I believe I shall be the victor of this tournament, for you are the greatest knight in the world."

"I know not of that," said Lancelot, "but I shall fight as best I can."

And so he went to the field and jousted

with such skill that he bested the three knights of the Round Table in the first minutes. Then he continued in the mock-battle, defeating all of the knights on the side of the king of North Wales. Before long, King Bagdemagus was declared the victor.

Once again, King Bagdemagus's daughter helped Lancelot from his horse. She thanked him, her eyes brimming with tears.

"You have brought me much honor to-day," King Bagdemagus said. "Please come inside and feast with us, and let me pay you with riches such as you deserve."

"I shall be glad to sup with you," Lancelot replied. "But I cannot accept any other payment, for my services here were part of a bargain between your daughter and myself, and we have each kept our part of it."

So Lancelot stayed and dined with King Bagdemagus and his daughter. But when the meal was completed, he pushed back from the table and continued on his journey. He found adventure and was victorious again and again, showing the world he was truly the greatest knight.

# Chapter 7

# The Kitchen Knight

QUEEN Morgause and King Lot of Orkney, Arthur's half sister and brother-in-law, had four sons. The youngest was called Gareth, and he was the handsomest of princes. Slim and broad-shouldered, Gareth stood a full head taller than all other men at his father's court. Even though Gareth was not yet a knight, he was more skilled and agile than most of the men who carried that title, beating everyone at mock jousts and battles with ease.

When Gareth was twenty years old, his mother called him to her side and told him that the time had come for him to go to Arthur's court. "You shall become a knight," she told him simply. And she sent him to her brother's court with three noble lords, a host of servants, and Gareth's own dwarf, Axatalese.

Gareth rode a beautiful white horse on a saddle of the finest leather, trimmed in gold. His clothing was of the softest gold velvet that shimmered in the sunlight. Surely his trappings alone would guarantee him knighthood.

After traveling a full day, the servants made camp for Gareth and the lords. The men enjoyed a succulent meal of meat and bread and wine, then everyone retired for the night.

Only Gareth tossed and turned. His mind was wide awake, thinking of a great many things. It came to him that he should not ride to his uncle the king's court with such pomp and circumstance. He should arrive only as himself, dressed in simple clothing and sitting on a plain leather saddle.

*For if I am truly worthy of knighthood,*

Gareth told himself, *I shall earn it through my deeds and not my bloodline.*

Very quietly, Gareth woke Axatalese and told him what to do. "Fetch me a plain saddle and clothing of simple green cloth. We shall go forward alone and arrive at my uncle's court in this way."

Axatalese did as he was told, and the two set out before dawn. When the lords and servants awoke several hours later, they were very dismayed to find Gareth gone. Terrified of telling the queen that her youngest son was missing, they fled to distant lands and were never seen in south Britain again.

Meanwhile, Gareth and his dwarf were arriving at Camelot. They rode up to the castle just as the feast of Pentecost was beginning. King Arthur had yet to sit down at the table. As was his custom, he did not do so until he had heard or seen something new and interesting.

While Axatalese saw to the horses,

Gareth strode into the great hall. Because Gareth dressed in a simple man's clothing, even his own brothers, Gawain, Gaheris, and Agravane, did not recognize him.

"Greetings, my good king," Gareth said with a bow. "I have traveled long and hard to be here and to ask of you two favors."

King Arthur gazed at the boy and saw great promise. For not only was he handsome and tall, his eyes were bright and full of intensity. "Ask, then," said the king.

"The first is that I may stay at your court for twelve full months and find my food and shelter here. As for the second, I will ask it when those twelve months have passed."

"If that is all you ask of me, then it shall be granted," replied Arthur. "And now tell me, what is your name?"

"I would pray you not make me tell you," Gareth replied. "Though in time you shall know."

Arthur nodded. "As you wish," he said.

For he enjoyed a bit of mystery and felt certain in his heart that this young man was much more than he appeared to be. "Sir Kay," Arthur called to his foster brother, who served the king as Camelot's chief steward, "see to it that our new friend is well fed and properly clothed."

"Yes, my lord," Kay replied. But he did not like the young man and did not see why his king should treat him so well. "I shall give him a name if he will not give himself one," Sir Kay said under his breath. "It shall be Beaumains," which means lovely hands, for his hands were as white and smooth as a woman's. "He will work and eat in the kitchens."

During the next twelve months, Sir Kay taunted Gareth at every opportunity. The kitchen workers also teased him at first, for he did not know how to handle a knife. Gareth took all of this teasing in stride, ignoring the rude remarks and making none in reply. He was a quick learner and was soon working more efficiently than those who had jeered at him.

Only two in Arthur's castle were truly kind to the kitchen knight: Lancelot and Gawain. Both offered to teach Gareth the knightly arts, for they saw him watching the jousts and sword fights whenever he could take leave of the kitchens. Gareth graciously thanked them both but declined their offers.

Finally, the twelve months had passed. It was once again the Pentecost feast, and Arthur was awaiting his bit of news before sitting down to dine.

He did not have to wait long. Soon a dark-haired damsel rushed into the hall and knelt before him.

"Pray, good king," she said, "I come in search of a knight who will be my sister's champion. She is imprisoned by the red knight of the Red Lands. He has burned her lands and now insists that she marry him, though she hates him with all her being."

King Arthur was about to reply when Gareth stepped forward. "Good king," he said, "I would that I might ask for my second favor, as twelve months have passed."

"Ask, then," said Arthur.

"I would like to be the champion of this damsel's sister," Gareth said.

The hall of knights suddenly grew quiet, and then laughter echoed off the walls.

Arthur did not laugh but simply gazed at the young man. In truth, he was not surprised by this request. "Your favor shall be granted," Arthur said.

The damsel scowled, for she saw that Gareth was dressed as a kitchen worker. "A kitchen knight?" she cried. "Here sit your famed knights of the Round Table, and you grant me the services of a kitchen knight? I would have a better chance of freeing my sister if I were to fight the red knight myself!" And the damsel turned on her heel, her black hair swinging behind her. She called for her horse, mounted, and raced away across the countryside.

Gareth was quick to follow. His dwarf had already readied his horse and armor and stood waiting in the courtyard. "Thank you, Axatalese," Gareth said as he dug his heels into his horse's flanks. Axatalese mounted his own mule, and together they left Camelot.

It did not take Gareth long to overtake the damsel.

"Away with you, kitchen knave," she said haughtily. "You are of no use to me, and you smell of grease and cooking."

Gareth heard a shrill laugh behind him and turned to see Sir Kay upon him. Sir Kay had followed the kitchen knight, intending to fight him and put him in his place.

He would be sorry that he did. For when the two men came crashing together, Gareth proved to be the stronger. He jabbed his sword into Sir Kay's shoulder, forcing him from his horse.

Now, it happened that Sir Lancelot had decided to follow Sir Kay. He knew the king's steward to be a bitter man and one with a strong anger toward the kitchen knight. He came upon the two men just as Gareth was putting Sir Kay back onto his horse and sending the animal homeward. Gareth kept only Sir Kay's spear, for he did not have one of his own.

"You fight well," Lancelot said to the young man as he halted his horse. "Better than many I have seen."

"Thank you," Gareth said. "I hope that one day I will be worthy of knighthood."

"That day has come," said Lancelot. "I know many a knight less worthy than you, and so I shall knight you now." Taking his sword, he tapped Gareth once on each shoulder, knighting him forever.

As Gareth felt the touch of Lancelot's sword, his heart lifted with joy.

"And now, tell me your name," Lancelot said.

"I shall whisper it," Gareth replied, "for I do not want this damsel to know my true identity." He leaned in close to Lancelot's ear.

"I am Gareth, son of King Lot and Queen Morgause of Orkney."

A smile played at the corners of Lancelot's mouth. "It is a small wonder that your own brothers, Gawain, Gaheris, and Agravane, did not recognize you when you came to Camelot," he said. "But I see that you are much younger than they, and perhaps they had not seen you in many a year."

"Nearly ten years," Gareth replied. "And I wanted to keep my identity a secret, even from my own kin."

"You have succeeded," Lancelot said.

"And I shall reveal nothing. I wish you luck in this adventure and with the damsel Linette, for that is her name."

With that, Lancelot leaped onto his horse and galloped away, dust stirring up under the horse's hooves.

Linette had seen all of this from a distance, but she had not heard her kitchen knight's name. "You may be a knight," she said when Gareth rode up to her, "but still you smell of stale food. Ride downwind of me so that I do not become ill from the stink of you."

Gareth was angry but stayed behind Linette without protest. In that way they rode on until they saw ahead of them a large tree with a twisted trunk and a black shield hanging from the branches. Beneath the tree sat a giant knight clad in black and sitting on a black horse.

"That is the black knight," Linette told Gareth. "You should flee from this place while you can."

"That I cannot do," replied Gareth, "for I have sworn to see this adventure through." And he rode on, a short distance behind Linette and in front of his dwarf.

When they came near him, the black knight's booming voice echoed over the countryside. "Is this your sister's champion, brought from Arthur's court?" he asked.

"Nay," Linette replied. "He is naught but a kitchen knave who follows me whether I wish him to or not."

"Then I shall have to fight him," said the black knight. Turning on Gareth, he said, "Make ready, for my spear is sharp."

While Linette rode on alone, the two men charged each other.

Crash! Their spears thrust against each other's shields with tremendous force. They exchanged blow after blow, and soon Gareth was wounded. But remembering the damsel's cruel words, Gareth fought on and brought the black knight down.

While the great knight lay moaning on the ground, Gareth took up his shield and mounted his horse.

"You shall ride to Camelot and pledge an oath to serve King Arthur," Gareth told the knight. "Tell him the kitchen knight sent you."

"I will do so," rasped the black knight. And Gareth turned and raced after the damsel.

"That was a strong knight you bested, but still you are nothing but a kitchen knave," Linette said when Gareth had caught up to her again. Yet Gareth thought that perhaps her words were not spoken quite as sharply as before.

"That is what you claim," he said. "Yet I have felled all the knights we have come across save Lancelot, who is my friend."

"That may be so, but it is by sheer luck that you have done so. Now, get down-wind of me, for I smell your kitchen filth."

Once again Gareth slowed his horse

and rode behind the damsel Linette without complaint. And so they traveled until they came to a giant field filled with a hundred blue pavilions.

"Surely, you will meet your death here, for this is the camp of the blue knight and all of the knights who follow him. Begone while you have the chance."

By this time, Gareth had grown weary of Linette's warnings and attempts to get rid of him. He did not answer her but simply rode onward, though it did occur to him that this warning seemed more sincere than the others, as if she did indeed fear for his life.

The knights of the blue knight camp came at Gareth one at a time. Swords flashed silver-blue in the sunlight as Gareth felled them all. Then the blue knight himself came forward to fight. It was a brutal battle, leaving both men breathless and wounded. Finally, the blue knight knelt before Gareth.

"You are the best knight I have fought, and I have fought many," he said. "My men and I shall serve you from this day forward."

"Then you shall serve King Arthur," said Gareth. "Go to him, and when you arrive in Camelot, tell the king that the kitchen knight sent you."

"Indeed, if that is your wish," said the blue knight. "My knights and I shall leave for Camelot in the morning. And now, please dine and rest the night with us. My squire will tend to your wounds."

Gareth was grateful for the food and drink and rest. Surprisingly, Linette did not scorn him to the blue knight but simply told him that they were riding to rescue her sister.

"Ah, it is she who is held captive by the red knight, in Castle Dangerous, just ten miles from here," said the blue knight. He turned toward Gareth. "May you rest well tonight, for it is not an easy battle that lies ahead."

"I am bound to do my best," said Gareth, "for I have pledged myself to be the lady's champion."

"You speak like a true and valiant knight," said the blue knight. Gareth did not reply but simply smiled at the Lady Linette.

Gareth slept soundly that night, and the next morning he and Linette continued to Castle Dangerous. They did not speak, but there was an easy silence between them, and Linette did not ask him to ride far behind her as before.

After a time, the castle came into view. Before it were several red pavilions spread across a grassy field. At the closest edge of the field stood a giant sycamore tree whose branches hung low with the bloodstained shields of many different knights.

"These are the shields of the knights who have come before you to fight for my sister," Linette said gravely. "None of them survived. I pray that you shall."

"I can only try," Gareth replied.

From the largest branch of the tree hung a giant ivory horn.

"Any who blows that horn must do battle with the red knight," said Linette. "But you should not blow until after the sun moves lower in the sky, for the red knight gains strength throughout the morning and weakens as the sun sets."

"I have come to fight for your sister, and I do not intend to wait," said Gareth. He took the great horn into his hands and blew, sending the sound toward Castle Dangerous.

It was not long before the red knight emerged, a giant covered head to toe in red armor and riding a russet horse.

As Sir Gareth watched the red knight approach, another sight held his attention. It was a beautiful damsel, with long golden hair, peering out from the highest window, her face lit with hope.

"That is my sister, the Lady Linesse," Linette said.

"I shall fight for her," said Gareth solemnly. And as he spoke, the red knight charged.

"Do not look at the lady, for she is mine!" he roared. "Look instead at the armor hanging from the sycamore, for yours will soon be among my collection!"

Gareth urged his horse into a gallop and charged the red knight. When the two knights came together, the sound echoed off the castle walls, bringing everyone within to the windows. Again the men came together, and with such force that their spears smashed into hundreds of pieces. They leaped to the ground, drawing their swords as they did so.

For an hour the two great knights exchanged blows, each hitting his mark more solidly than before. More than once the castle dwellers thought the men must have broken their necks because they fell to the ground with tremendous force. Never before had they seen such a fierce fight. Indeed, the opponents seemed more like lions than men.

Finally, just before noon, the red knight struck Gareth with such a blow that the kitchen knight's sword clattered to the ground.

Linette gasped. "Sir Gareth, you must find strength, for my sister is watching you!"

Gareth pulled himself up, grabbed his sword, and threw himself at the red knight with every ounce of his being. Knocking the red knight's weapon from his grasp, Gareth wrestled him to the ground and fiercely tore off his helmet.

"I yield!" cried the red knight. "Pray, let me live!"

Gareth sheathed his sword, and the red knight staggered to his feet.

"You and all your followers shall immediately begin your journey to Camelot to pledge your service to Arthur, our king," Gareth said. "And you shall tell him that you were sent by the kitchen knight."

"Agreed," said the red knight.

"And you shall beg the forgiveness of the lady you have kept in the tower," Gareth added.

The red knight hung his head in shame. "Agreed," he said again.

"And you shall vow to treat all ladies with gentleness and virtue from this day onward," Gareth finished.

"I shall," said the red knight. He went to the window where Linesse still stood and begged her forgiveness on his knees. When she had forgiven him, the red knight and his men left Castle Dangerous for Camelot.

Only after the red knight departed did Gareth realize how badly he was wounded and how tired he felt. Axatalese helped him into one of the red pavilions and bathed him and applied salve to his wounds. Then Gareth fell into a deep sleep.

Meanwhile, inside the castle, Linette and her sister, Linesse, embraced each other happily, for their days of peril were over.

"Tell me, good sister," said Linesse, "who is this knight who has saved me?"

"That I cannot tell you, for I know him only as a kitchen knave of Arthur's court. When I requested the help of one of Arthur's knights, none save he offered his services. But I can tell you that throughout our journey he behaved as a man of high and noble blood, despite my treatment of him. For I scorned his kitchen smell and his lowly rank. You as well as I saw him defeat the red knight, as he did the others who came across our path."

"He is most assuredly a man of worth, for he risked his own life to save mine. I care not whether he is of noble blood, yet in truth I would like to know his name."

Suddenly, Linette's eyes gleamed. "Axatalese!" she cried. And she quickly left the chamber.

Linette found Axatalese just outside his master's pavilion. She bade him follow her, and he did so willingly.

"Axatalese," said Linette when she had returned to Linesse's chamber, "we wish no harm upon you. My sister would simply like to know the name of the good knight who has rescued her."

Axatalese bowed slightly. "This knight is Sir Gareth of Orkney, son of King Lot and Queen Morgause, sister to the king."

When Linette heard this, no words could escape her mouth. For though she had begun to suspect he was of noble blood, she had not thought that he was nephew to the king himself! Linesse also said nothing, but a radiant smile spread across her lovely face.

When the sun rose the next morning, Linesse went to Gareth and thanked him for rescuing her. As she knelt by his bedside she was so beautiful that Gareth fell instantly in love with her. As she tended his wounds and talked with him throughout the long days of recovery, she fell in love with him as well. Linette watched the two of them and was happy, for she knew that they were made for each other.

Soon Gareth was well again, and Gareth, Axatalese, Linette, and Linesse traveled together to Camelot. On their journey Linette told her sister of their journey to Castle Dangerous and of Gareth's bravery. And when they arrived at Camelot, Gareth was welcomed in honor, embraced by his brothers, and given his rightful seat at the Round Table.

# Chapter 8

# The Loathly Lady

CHRISTMAS in King Arthur's court was celebrated over many weeks. After a time of reflection came a time of great merrymaking and joyous festivities that lasted until January. Then the season was capped off with the largest party of all to welcome in the New Year.

For weeks, Camelot had been alive with poems and songs, feasting and fun. But on the eve of the New Year the great hall was decked like never before and filled to the rafters with food, music, and revelers. Arthur enjoyed the feasting and merriment as he always did, but more than ever he enjoyed the company of his knights. Each evening after dinner one or another of the knights would stand before the court, recounting his adventures of the last year.

The countless acts of bravery, valor, courtesy, and kindness swelled King Arthur's heart with pride. But in the back of his mind was another feeling. Arthur had been too long at Camelot and craved an adventure of his own.

Almost as soon as Arthur realized what he was feeling there came a great clattering of hooves in the courtyard. Weeping and covered in mud and bruises, a fair damsel threw herself on the mercy of the company.

"You must help me," she sobbed. "You must save my love."

Arthur knelt beside the girl and dried her tears. He beckoned his squires to bring food and wine to sustain the poor maiden. Then he coaxed the terrible tale from her.

"I was riding north with my love when

we came upon a dark lake surrounded by rocks," she began. "And in the middle of the lake was a great castle with black flags flying high over its towers. We wished to pass unharmed, but before we could go by, the drawbridge was lowered and an evil knight riding a horse with eyes like fire came thundering toward us. The knight was bigger than two men and demanded that my love yield and surrender me to him." The maiden's hands trembled as she took a sip of wine.

"Of course my love refused. He drew his sword to defend me, but then a strange magic came over him. He could not move, and I was powerless to save him."

The damsel's tears began to flow again as she continued her tale. "The wizard knight slung my love over his saddle as easily as one slings a fox fresh from the hunt.

"I ordered that he release my love in

King Arthur's name, but the wizard knight only laughed. I swore I would come to King Arthur's court and seek a champion, perhaps the king himself!" The girl's voice grew quiet. "The only reply he gave was his terrible laugh as he rode back across the bridge. In my head I hear the laughter still."

King Arthur was outraged. He sprang to his feet and spoke in a loud voice. "By my honor, the king *will* ride upon this matter."

Many of the knights cheered for their lord. The poor maiden's wrongs must be avenged! But Gawain stood in defiance.

"My lord, I sense some evil afoot," he said humbly. "Allow me to quest in your place. Britain cannot afford to lose her king."

Hearing Gawain, Lancelot, Kay, Bedivere, and several others also offered to take Arthur's place. But the king had made up his mind.

The next morning, with Excalibur at his side, Arthur rode with the maiden in the direction whence she came. By the time they reached the rocky lake and the black castle, the sky was beginning to darken.

Arthur called out once, twice, three times, and when no one answered he shouted over the castle wall. "Sir knight, it is I, Arthur Pendragon, your king. Do not keep me waiting."

At last, the drawbridge was lowered to reveal the wizard knight, just as the damsel had described. Seated atop his fire-eyed warhorse, he answered the king's challenge.

"Welcome," the knight shouted. "I have often wished I could do battle with you. For you are not my king. You are nothing but a coward."

Hearing this, Arthur's anger flared. He prodded his horse and rode at the wizard knight at a full gallop. He shouted for the knight to yield as he readied his lance.

The wizard knight showed no sign of yielding and instead spurred his own horse. But before Arthur's lance struck the other's shield, Arthur's horse stopped in its tracks. Arthur was nearly flung into the lake.

Arthur's horse whinnied and trembled beneath him. For the first time, the king sensed the evil Sir Gawain had warned him of. There was magic afoot. Dark magic.

Suddenly, the air was filled with a horrible sound — the sound of the wizard knight's laughter. It echoed across the lake and stopped only when the wizard knight spoke.

"It is not I who must yield, it is you," he spat. "Yield or fight!"

Arthur tried to reach his sword and found that he could not even raise his arm. He willed his muscles to work but could not move. He was frozen.

The wizard knight threw back his head

and laughed again. "I could kill you now or throw you in my dungeon to rot. Instead, I offer you this: You can buy your freedom if you can answer one question."

"What question is that?" Arthur growled. He did not like to bargain, but he had no choice.

The knight spoke slowly, as if Arthur were dim-witted. "What is it that all women most desire?" he asked. Then he turned his horse and shouted over his shoulder. "Return to me in one week's time with or without the answer."

As soon as the wizard knight's back was turned, Arthur's horse spooked. It jumped free of the spell and ran as fast as it could through the trees. It was some time before Arthur could slow the beast to a walk. When he finally did, the maiden who had led him to the wizard knight was nowhere to be found. Arthur realized that he had been tricked into battle with the wizard knight.

For the next week, Arthur rode alone. He asked the wizard knight's question of each woman he came across, be she young or old, rich or poor. Never once did he get the same answer.

"Riches," said one.

"Beauty," said another.

Laughter, love, power, and family were all among the answers he heard. Carefully, he memorized every one, though he knew deep down none was the answer the wizard knight was looking for.

On the evening of the last day, Arthur headed back to the castle in the lake with a heavy heart. He wished Merlin the Wise were there to help him. Even though the good wizard had been asleep for many years, Arthur had never grown entirely accustomed to making decisions without his thoughtful counsel.

Lost in thought, Arthur barely heard when a woman wearing a hooded cloak and sitting under a tree called out to him.

"Good evening, my lord King Arthur."

The king nearly fell from his horse when he paused to return the greeting. The woman's voice was sweet, but her appearance was horrid. The shock of it was so great all Arthur could do was stare with an open mouth.

Her skin was as dry as old leaves. Her long nose bent to the side, and her pointed, hairy chin stuck out so far Arthur failed to notice that she squinted at him through only one good eye.

In spite of her haggard appearance, the woman was dressed in rich fabrics, and on her gnarled hands she had jewels worthy of Arthur's own queen.

Arthur was silent as he took this all in.

"What kind of a knight are you that you do not return a lady's greeting?" the woman scolded. "Mind your manners, sir, for I know what errand you are on, and if you are kind I might be of some help."

"Forgive me." Arthur bowed. "I was lost

in my own thoughts. If indeed you can help me with the question I must answer, answer quickly and I will be forever grateful."

"I seek more than gratitude," the lady said.

"Whatever you want you shall have," the king answered hastily.

The loathly lady made the king swear to his promise. Then she beckoned him nearer with one twisted finger. "Come closer," she breathed. When the king was close enough to feel the heat of her body, she whispered in his ear. The moment he heard it, Arthur knew that the loathly lady had given him the answer he was looking for.

"How can I repay you?" he asked, smiling for the first time in days.

"When you have given your answer to the wizard knight and are sure that it is the right one, I will be waiting here to tell you what I desire," the lady replied.

Satisfied and feeling much lighter, the king rode on to the wizard's castle. He arrived as night was falling, just as he had before, but this time he did not need to call out. The wizard knight was waiting for him on the bridge.

"Did you bring the answer to my question?" The knight smirked.

"I brought many answers," Arthur said calmly. Then he listed each one save the one he'd gotten from the loathly lady. As he ticked them off on his fingers the wizard knight began to laugh. It started as a chuckle and deepened into a thunderous roar with a more grating sound behind it, like breaking glass. When the wizard knight was laughing so hard he seemed in danger of falling off his horse, Arthur stopped.

"Now you will yield to me, Arthur Pendragon." The wizard knight sneered and put his hand on the hilt of his sword. "And the rule of Britain shall be mine."

"Not just yet," Arthur said calmly. "I have one more answer."

"Very well," the wizard knight said.

"The thing that every woman desires most is . . . her own way."

The wizard knight bellowed in anger, a scream much worse than his laughter. "Go!" he roared. "That is the right answer, and you are free. But it was my sister who told you, and if ever I find her she will die in flames."

Arthur rode away from the wizard knight and back to the loathly lady. "Good woman," he said, "I have you to thank for my life and my kingdom. Now, what favor will you have in return? Ask and you shall have it."

"I pray, King Arthur, that you are a man of your word," the lady spoke. "The thing that I desire is for one of your good knights to take me as his beloved bride."

Arthur felt the wind go out of his lungs.

How could he force one of his knights to marry a woman so ugly? It was impossible.

The loathly lady saw the surprise on Arthur's face, and the glimmer of hope in her one good eye was snuffed out. "You made a promise, Arthur Pendragon," she scolded.

"And I will keep it," Arthur said, sitting up in his saddle. But when he turned his horse to home he was filled with dread.

Before the court, Arthur told the tale of his adventure. "I am badly beaten," he finished, hanging his head.

"Sir, you gave the wizard knight the right answer and stand before us whole and unscarred. How is it that you are beaten?" Lancelot asked.

"I would be under the power of the wizard knight without the help of one woman. She gave me the right answer and bought my freedom. But the price I must pay for that answer is great, and I cannot pay it myself," the king explained.

"What is the price?" Gawain demanded.

"That one of my knights take her as his wife," Arthur said.

"That is no great price," Gawain scoffed. "We might all benefit from a fair bride!"

"But she is not fair," Arthur said gravely. "Far from it. She is the most hideous person I have ever laid eyes upon. The only thing more twisted than her face is her gruesome body, and she sees the world through one slit of an eye. I wish that I could repay this promise myself, but I cannot," Arthur said with a glance toward Guenevere.

The single knights at court spoke to one another under their breath, and those with wives and families sat silent and grateful.

"It is up to your loyal knights to keep your honor," Gawain's brother Agravane spoke up. Agravane was a prankster and

120

loved to goad his older brother's temper. "Gawain is single. It is a pity he is too poor a knight to champion you, my lord."

Just as Agravane intended, the fire was fanned in Gawain. His anger flared and he leaped up. "My lord, I would be happy to wed the woman and keep your word and honor."

Arthur saw that Gawain had been tricked into agreeing to take the woman as his wife. He told Gawain that he would not hold him to his offer until he had seen the loathly lady with his own eyes.

"Then let us find her at once," Gawain said, pounding the table and glaring at Agravane. "I am eager for my wedding day."

A short time later, a whole fleet of knights rode out of the courtyard and into the forest in search of the loathly lady. Although Gawain was the only one who had thoughts of marriage, the others were curious to see the misshapen maid. The party brought hounds and huntsmen with them so they could hunt along the way.

They had taken two deer before anyone caught a glimpse of the woman in the woods. It was Sir Kay who spied her at last. He alerted the others, then stood before the loathly lady, too shocked to speak and a little afraid. Turning to the other knights as they galloped up, he spoke rudely, "I see now why the lady must find a husband thus. Who could look upon her daily? Who, I ask, could kiss her horrible mouth?"

"Silence, Sir Kay," the king reprimanded Kay angrily. "That is no way for a knight to speak of a lady."

Kay was silenced, and the rest of the knights held their tongues. They felt sorry for the woman and would not dream of mocking her, as Kay had. Instead, they turned their heads away and shifted in their saddles uncomfortably.

Gawain did not. He looked evenly at the woman and saw something in her the others missed. He did not feel pity but something different. Something he could not name.

"Why so quiet, friends?" he asked the hunting party. "Is this not a joyous occasion? I have come to ask this woman to be my wife!" Gawain dismounted and knelt before the loathly lady. "If she will have me."

The woman offered Gawain her hand. "Sir Gawain, I am the Lady Ragnell," she said.

"Dear lady, will you take me as your husband?" Gawain asked, touching his lips to her withered hand.

"If your asking is true," she said. "But think hard on this. Will you be happy wed to a woman as old and ugly as I am? You are young and courageous and handsome. Am I a fitting bride for you, the king's own nephew? What will the lords and ladies of the court say when they see me?"

"They will show you courtesy or face my wrath," Gawain said, never dropping her hand.

Lady Ragnell began to cry, and it did nothing to improve her looks. "I will bring shame to you, Sir Gawain," she wailed.

"I can protect myself as well as you," Gawain said as he dried her good eye. "Come now, we must go and prepare for our wedding."

Gawain lifted the woman ahead of him on his horse, and the entire party rode back toward the castle. The wedding was to be held that very night, but the usual joking and merriment at such an occasion was strangely absent.

As they rode through the streets outside the castle walls, the peasants saw Lady Ragnell and shrunk back in fear. Inside the castle walls, Guenevere and the ladies of the court were more kind. But even they were unable to hide their dismay at the lady's appearance.

When Lady Ragnell walked down the church aisle to meet her husband, most of the lords and ladies stared straight ahead to avoid looking into her hideous face. Only Gawain looked her in the eye. All evening, Lady Ragnell's new husband was at her side, through the feasting and the dancing and the telling of tales. But it was painfully clear that Gawain was the only one, except for King Arthur, who was able to look upon the lady as though nothing were wrong.

The uncomfortable evening finally came to a close. The castle servants escorted the bride and groom to their chambers. A fire flickered in the fireplace, and Gawain collapsed, exhausted, into a chair beside it.

"Have you nothing to say, my love?" the lady asked, standing beside him.

Gawain watched the flames dance and listened to his wife's sweet voice and thought about the day's events.

"Will you not look at me now?" she asked.

Gawain shifted his gaze and fell out of his chair in astonishment. The woman standing beside him wearing his bride's gown and jewels was the most beautiful maiden he had ever seen. Gone were the twisted mouth, gouged eye, and bearded chin. And in their place was skin as smooth as silk, soft, curling hair, two round green eyes, and a smiling rosebud of a mouth.

Gawain shook his head to wake from dreaming. "Where is my wife, the Lady Ragnell?" he asked.

"Here before you," the lady replied. "I am the bride whom you wedded for your king. Your kindness has broken a spell that was put upon me, but it is only partly broken.

"Now for a time you can look upon my true form. Are you not pleased?"

"Pleased indeed," Gawain stammered. "I have saved my king's honor and gained a prize greater than my imaginings. From the moment I saw you I felt a calling. I did not know what it was, but now I am the happiest husband in Camelot."

Gawain reached out to take his bride in his arms, but she held him off.

"Wait, my beloved, because the spell is still not all undone." The lady held Gawain's large hands in her own. "You have a choice to make, and it will not be an easy one. I can only be fair by day or by night. You must choose whether you will have the world see me as I stand before you now or if you would save this true form for yourself in our private chambers."

"Save your beauty for me," Gawain said hastily. Then he stopped himself. "Wait." He paced before the fire. The choice was harder than he thought. He remembered the lords and ladies of the court, unable to meet his lady's eye. Why should she be pitied and humiliated when she was truly more lovely than any of them?

"I was thinking of myself," Gawain apologized, taking hold of the lady's hands. "If it will make you happier you must be lovely by day. I will know your true self even behind the hideous form."

"Your answer is sweet," the lady replied. "But you mean more to me than the king's court."

"Then you must choose yourself, my lady," Gawain said. "For you are the one who knows best what will make you happy. Whatever pleases you most will also please me."

Lady Ragnell collapsed onto Gawain's chest. A noise rose from her throat that was a sob and a laugh all at once. "Dear Gawain! My love. My lord. By granting me my own way you have broken the spell completely! I am free to appear as myself night and day."

Lady Ragnell explained to Gawain that she and her brother, the wizard knight, had both fallen under the power of Morgana le Fay. As part of a plot to kill King Arthur, Morgana put them under a spell so strong it was nearly impossible for humans to break it. But break it Gawain had, in the name of love for his king, his country, and his wife.

The next day, everyone was happy to see Gawain and his lovely new bride, especially King Arthur. But none was happier than the bride and groom themselves. The Lady Ragnell's love even helped to cool Gawain's hot temper. And they lived together happily for many years to come.

# Epilogue

KING Arthur's reign was long and glorious. He brought law and order to the good people of Britain, kept the country's borders safe, and established the most famous brotherhood of knights in all the world.

Arthur's countless adventures and noble good deeds made him much beloved throughout his kingdom. Many began to believe that Arthur's reign might last forever — but Morgana le Fay still sought her revenge.

In yet another plot to destroy her half brother, Morgana sent her son, Mordred, to become a knight in King Arthur's court. Arthur welcomed the boy as family. But when the king was away, Mordred betrayed him and seized the throne. Too late, Arthur realized that Mordred was up to no good. He returned to face Morgana's son on the battlefield. After a brutal fight, the king succeeded in killing the traitor. But before he died, Mordred inflicted Arthur with a mortal wound.

After King Arthur died, dark days returned to Britain. In the hardest times, stories of the noble king were told and retold, giving hope to the people and brightening the darkness.

Some still believe that King Arthur is not truly dead, but merely sleeping, hidden under the lapping waters in the castle of the Lady of the Lake. Whether that be truth or legend, King Arthur and his knights of the Round Table are alive in the memories and hearts of those who hear and tell his story. In this way, he shall live forever.

# Classic Editions of Timeless Tales...for Today's Readers

## Junior Classics

| | | |
|---|---|---|
| ☐ BFC 0-439-23621-5 | *Robinson Crusoe* | $3.99 US |
| ☐ BFC 0-439-23620-7 | *Gulliver's Stories* | $3.99 US |
| ☐ BFC 0-439-23641-X | *The Wizard of Oz* | $3.99 US |
| ☐ BFC 0-439-23639-8 | *Robin Hood of Sherwood Forest* | $3.99 US |
| ☐ BFC 0-439-29149-6 | *Alice in Wonderland* | $4.50 US |
| ☐ BFC 0-439-44774-2 | *Wind in the Willows* | $4.50 US |
| ☐ BFC 0-439-22510-8 | *The Legend of Sleepy Hollow* | $3.99 US |
| ☐ BFC 0-439-29154-2 | *Paul Bunyan and Other Tall Tales* | $3.99 US |
| ☐ BFC 0-439-22506-X | *Heidi* | $3.99 US |
| ☐ BFC 0-439-29145-3 | *The Little Mermaid and Other Stories* | $3.99 US |